W9-CMQ-142

DATE DUE

SEP 2 5 2015		
OCT 2 1 2015		
NOV 1 0 2015		
DEC 2 9 2015		
JUL 1 2 2016		

PRINTED IN U.S.A.

A CAT IS CHASING ME THROUGH THIS BOOK!
is published by Picture Window Books,
A Capstone Imprint
1710 Roe Crest Drive
North Mankato, Minnesota 56003
www.capstonepub.com

Copyright © 2014 Turner Entertainment Co.
Tom and Jerry and all related characters
and elements are trademarks of and © Turner Entertainment Co.
WB SHIELD: ™ & © Warner Bros. Entertainment Inc.
(s15)

CAPS32944

All rights reserved. No part of this publication may be
reproduced in whole or in part, or stored in a retrieval system,
or transmitted in any form or by any means, electronic,
mechanical, photocopying, recording, or otherwise, without
written permission of the publisher.

Library of Congress Cataloging-in-Publication Data
is available on the Library of Congress website.
ISBN: 978-1-62370-126-0 (paper over board)
ISBN: 978-1-4795-5229-0 (library hardcover)
ISBN: 978-1-4795-6161-2 (eBook)

DESIGNED BY:
Russell Griesmer

ILLUSTRATED BY:
Comicup Studio
Carmen Pérez — Pencils
Francesc Figueres Farrès — Inks
Gloria Caballe — Color

Printed in the United States of America in North Mankato, Minnesota.
042014   008087CGF14

A CAT IS CHASING ME THROUGH THIS BOOK!

by Benjamin Bird

WEST BRIDGEWATER PUBLIC LIBRARY

PICTURE WINDOW BOOKS
capstonepub.com

WEST BRIDGEWATER PUBLIC LIBRARY

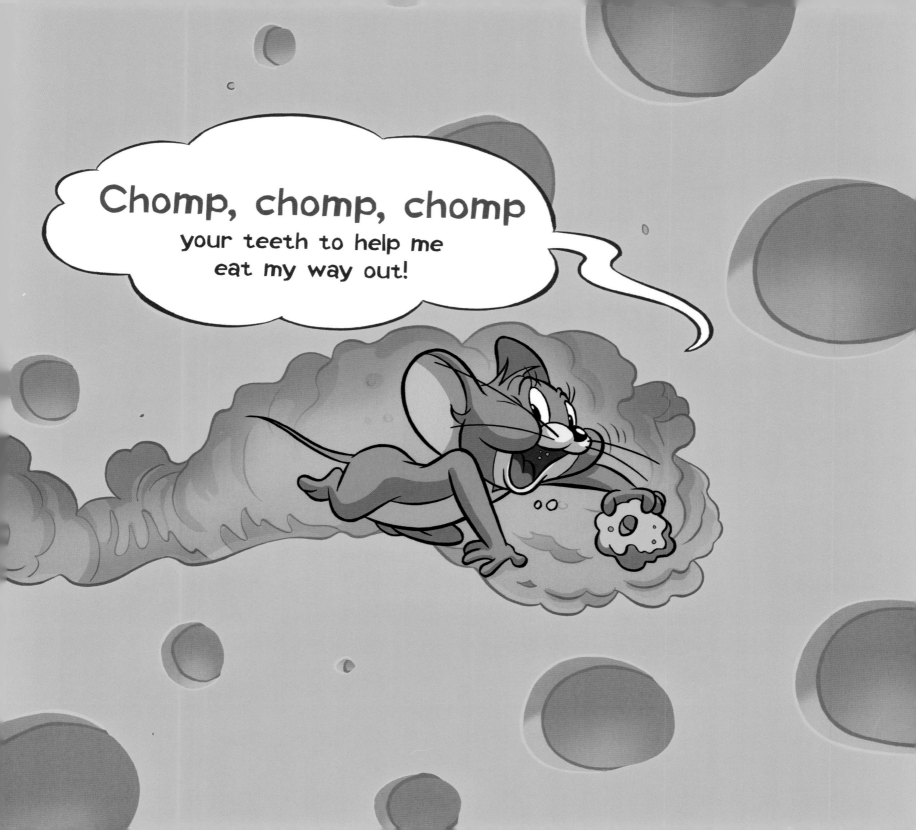